Hello, Family Members,

Learning to read is one of the most important accomplishments of early childhood. **Hello Reader!** books are designed to help children become skilled readers who like to read. Beginning readers learn to read by remembering frequently used words like "the," "is," and "and"; by using phonics skills to decode new words; and by interpreting picture and text clues. These books provide both the stories children enjoy and the structure they need to read fluently and independently. Here are suggestions for helping your child *before*, *during*, and *after* reading:

Before

- Look at the cover and pictures and have your child predict what the story is about.
- Read the story to your child.
- Encourage your child to chime in with familiar words and phrases.
- Echo read with your child by reading a line first and having your child read it after you do.

During

- Have your child think about a word he or she does not recognize right away. Provide hints such as "Let's see if we know the sounds" and "Have we read other words like this one?"
- Encourage your child to use phonics skills to sound out new words.
- Provide the word for your child when more assistance is needed so that he or she does not struggle and the experience of reading with you is a positive one.
- Encourage your child to have fun by reading with a lot of expression . . . like an actor!

After

- Have your child keep lists of interesting and favorite words.
- Encourage your child to read the books over and over again. Have him or her read to brothers, sisters, grandparents, and even teddy bears. Repeated readings develop confidence in young readers.
- Talk about the stories. Ask and answer questions. Share ideas about the funniest and most interesting characters and events in the stories.

I do hope that you and your child enjoy this book.

> —Francie Alexander
> Reading Specialist,
> Scholastic's Instructional Publishing Group

If you have questions or comments about how children learn to read, please contact Francie Alexander at FrancieAl@aol.com

*With thanks to Charlie and Willy Lent,
and the real Coach Cooper
— J.M.*

*To Sophie, Sadie, and Rhett
— T.K.*

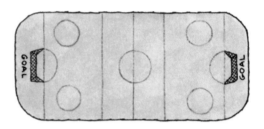

Go to www.scholastic.com for Web site information
on Scholastic authors and illustrators.

Text copyright © 1998 by Jean Marzollo.
Illustrations copyright © 1998 by True Kelley.
All rights reserved. Published by Scholastic Inc.
HELLO READER! and CARTWHEEL BOOKS and associated logos
are trademarks and/or registered trademarks of Scholastic Inc.

Library of Congress Cataloging-in-Publication Data

Marzollo, Jean.
    Hockey hero / by Jean Marzollo; illustrated by True Kelley.
        p.   cm. — (Hello reader! Level 3)
    Summary: When Hal moves to a new town where he is no longer
the star hockey player, he learns that scoring goals is not the only way
to be a star.
    ISBN 0-590-38397-3
    [1. Hockey — Fiction.   2. Cooperativeness — Fiction.]
I. Kelley, True, ill.   II. Title.   III. Series.
PZ7.M3688Ho   1998
[E] — dc21   97-19281
                                                                              CIP
                                                                              AC

10 9 8 7 6 5 4 3 2 1   8 9/9 0/0 01 02
                            Printed in the U.S.A.   24
                            First printing, December 1998

Hockey Hero

by Jean Marzollo and Dan Marzollo
Illustrated by True Kelley

Hello Reader! — Level 3

SCHOLASTIC INC. Cartwheel B·O·O·K·S ®
New York   Toronto   London   Auckland   Sydney

Hal stood up and looked around the rink.

"Can you help me?" said a voice. "My name's Joey."

Hal looked down. Joey was the smallest kid on the team.

"Will you lace up my skates?" asked Joey.

"Can't you do it by yourself?" asked Hal.

"I can't get them tight enough," said Joey.

Hal knelt down. He laced up Joey's skates.
Inside, Hal was worried. The kids on his
new team looked so young!

Coach Cooper gave the team a pep talk. "Amanda, watch for passes. Matt, stay in front of the net. Everybody go for the puck."

Hal couldn't wait to start skating. He tapped his stick on the floor.

"Hal," said the coach, "this is your first time with us. Welcome to the Flyers!"

Coach Cooper turned to the other players. "Hal just moved to town," she said. "His dad told me that he's played a lot of hockey. He's going to start at center today. Maybe he will help us beat the Penguins!"

They skated out on the ice.

Hal and the Penguin center stood face to face in the center of the rink.

The referee dropped the puck between them. Hal hit the puck and raced down the ice. He streaked by Penguins trying to protect their goal. *Bam!* Hal shot the puck toward the net.

But the puck didn't go *into* the net. It hit
the Penguin goalie's chest pad. Hal couldn't
believe it. He had *not* scored.

This was embarrassing.

Meanwhile, the Penguins moved the
puck back to the Flyers' goal.

Hal chased after them. Most of the Penguins were on one side. Matt, the Flyers' goalie, moved toward them. "Don't go too far!" shouted Hal.

But it was too late. A smart Penguin
passed the puck across the ice. Another
Penguin shot it into the net.

The score was now Penguins 1, Flyers 0.

Hal wanted to show his new team how
good he was. He skated with the puck back
down the ice.

"Pass, pass!" yelled the coach.

But Hal didn't pass. He wanted to score
by himself. He lifted his stick. He took
careful aim. And then . . .

He fell down. Joey fell on top of him.

"What happened?" asked Hal. "Did you knock me down?"

"I didn't mean to!" cried Joey. "I couldn't stop. I'm sorry."

"Where's the puck?" asked Hal.

The Penguins were passing it back and forth down the ice. The Penguins scored. The score was now Penguins 2, Flyers 0.

I don't believe this, said Hal to himself. *Our goalie stinks. Joey stinks. And I stink worst of all.*

The game never got better for the Flyers. When it ended, the score was still Penguins 2, Flyers 0.

"Cheer up," said Hal's dad afterward.
"Let's go get some double fudge ice cream."
In their old town, they went with the team
to the ice cream parlor after every game.

"I bet there's no ice cream parlor in this
stupid town," said Hal. He wished they had
never moved. But wishing didn't help.

"Every town has ice cream," said Hal's
dad. He stopped at a little store and got a
quart of double fudge.

At home, they ate in silence. The ice cream tasted great, but Hal still felt rotten.

"The next game will be better," said his dad. Hal's dad had been a hockey star in college. He didn't play anymore, but he went to all of Hal's games.

"Joey knocked me over," said Hal.

"Don't worry about Joey," said his dad. "Worry about yourself. You're the best player on the team. Next game? I bet you'll get a hat trick."

On Hal's old team, he had gotten many hat tricks.

"I bet I'll get two hat tricks," said Hal. He felt better now.

A hat trick is when a player scores three goals in one game.

At the next game, the Flyers played the Flames. As Hal laced up Joey's skates, he gave Joey a warning.

DON'T RUN INTO ME AGAIN.

Hal was determined. He skated faster than everyone. He got the puck as often as he could. He tried again and again to score.

But he couldn't. Sometimes the puck hit the goalie. Sometimes it sailed right over the goal.

"Pass, pass!" yelled Coach Cooper.

But Hal didn't listen. The score was 0–0. Hal kept trying to score, and he kept missing. Something was wrong. The harder he tried, the worse he got.

The game was almost over. The score was still 0–0. Hal was upset. *Forget the hat trick,* he told himself. *Just get one goal. Win the game for the Flyers.*

Hal stole the puck from a Flame player. "Shoot!" his dad yelled.

Hal was in front of the goal. It was now or never! Hal slapped the puck. *Ding!* It hit the crossbar and bounced in front of Joey. Joey quickly hit it into the goal.

Score!

The buzzer sounded. The game was over. The Flyers had won.

Everyone congratulated Joey.

At home, Hal said, "I think I'm in a slump."

"There's no such thing as a slump," said his dad. "Think positive. At the next game, you'll score."

But in the next game, Hal did not score. The Flyers lost.

After the game, Hal collapsed on the bench. He held back tears. He still had not scored one goal on his new team.

Coach Cooper sat down next to him. "Hockey isn't just about offense. It isn't just about scoring," she said. "It's also about defense. It's about stopping the other team from scoring. Hal, you are a fine defensive player. Next game, Jamie will take your place at center. You'll play defense."

"Coach, you can't do that!" said Hal.

"Yes, she can," said a voice. It was Hal's father. "She's the coach," he said. "She makes the decisions."

"I'll never become a star playing defense," said Hal.

"You'll never become a star unless you start enjoying yourself," said Coach Cooper.

"How can I enjoy myself if I'm not scoring?" asked Hal on the way home.

"Do you like to steal the puck?" asked his dad.

"Sure," said Hal.

"Do you like to skate around other players?" asked his dad.

"Of course," said Hal.

"Now you'll be able to enjoy those moments," said his dad.

"I doubt it," said Hal.

At the next game, the other Flyers were surprised.

"You're not playing center anymore?" asked Joey.

"Things change," said Hal. "It's about time you changed, too. Lace up your own skates."

"No way!" cried Joey. "You bring me good luck! I scored a goal wearing skates you laced!"

Hal had to admit that Joey was playing better. "Okay then," said Hal, "I'll tie yours if you tie mine. See if you can bring *me* luck."

"We sure need luck today," said Joey. "The Rangers are the best."

Hal wanted *his* team to be the best.

Out on the ice, Hal stole the puck from a Ranger. Next, he skated with it toward the goal. Then he faked a shot toward the goal and passed the puck to Amanda.

Amanda scored.

The Flyers were ahead 1–0. Hal smiled. His dad was right. Hal could enjoy himself without having to score!

Hal set up goals for Jamie and then
for Joey. They both scored. The Flyers
beat the Rangers 3–0.

Hal was proud of himself. His defensive play had helped his team win.

Joey hugged him. So did Amanda. So did Jamie. So did Coach Cooper. So did his dad!

Hal felt like a hero.

"Is there an ice cream parlor in town?" his dad asked.

"Sure is," said Coach Cooper. "There's one on Main Street. Why?"

"I'd like to invite the whole team there to celebrate the victory," he said.

All the kids cheered. Especially Hal.

Hal ordered a hot fudge sundae with whipped cream and a cherry on top. So did his teammates. So did Coach Cooper and his dad. For the first time, Hal felt at home in his new town.